The Hidden Secret

Copyright

The suspense is much important
in life,

To keep moving forward.

The secrets are hidden,

Are just found in documents,

This may be caught by a person,

Who may take it positively or

negatively?

Acknowledgements

I extend my deepest gratitude to Mr K.K. Yadav, Principal of JNV Solan, for his unwavering support and guidance. A special thanks to my English teachers, the library teacher, and all other teachers who have enriched my learning experience.

I am immensely grateful to my previous school, Gurukul International Sr. Sec. School Solan, for promoting my love for English and providing a strong foundation.

To my parents, words cannot fully express my appreciation for your unwavering support and encouragement throughout this journey. Your belief in me has been the cornerstone of my success, and your constant love and guidance have kept me grounded and motivated. Thank you for always being there, cheering me on, and providing me with the strength to pursue my dreams.

To my brother, my relatives, and everyone who has supported me along the way, I am deeply thankful for your encouragement and faith in my abilities.

I would also like to express my appreciation to my schoolmates and friends Kriti Katna and Sejal Negi for their companionship and motivation. My heartfelt thanks go to my seniors, Trisha, Bhoomika, Tamanna, Sneha, and Pragya, for their guidance and support.

Disclaimer

This book is a work of fiction. The characters, events, and locations depicted in this novel are creations of the author's imagination. Any resemblance to real persons, living or dead, or to real events or places, is entirely coincidental.

The mysterious room owned by Henry and the relationships he forms with the five characters are purely fictional. The depiction of Joseph as the not-so-good Principal of St. Mary's School in Shimla is a product of the author's imagination.

Readers should not interpret the settings, events, or any actions of the characters in this story as reflections of real-life situations or personalities. Any similar names, places, or occurrences are unintended and coincidental.

Prologue

In the picturesque town of Shimla, nestled in the misty hills, stood the historic St. Mary's School. The grandeur of its old stone buildings masked the secrets that lay hidden within its walls. The school was known not only for its academic excellence but also for the eerie tales that whispered through its hallways.

One such tale was about Henry, a former student who had discovered a secret room within the school. Over the years, this room had become a place of solace for Henry, a sanctuary from the outside world. Unbeknownst to most, this room held a power that could alter the very fabric of reality.

Then there was Joseph, the Principal of St. Mary's School. On the surface, he was a stern and authoritative figure, but behind his façade laid a malevolent intent. His dark ambitions and the lengths he would go to achieve them were known to very few.

The story unfolds when five students—Aayan, Aarya, Daisy, Roy, and Trisha—stumble upon the secret room and form an unlikely alliance with Henry. As they unravel the mysteries of the room and uncover the sinister truth about Joseph, they realize they are in a race against time. Their journey is one of courage, friendship, and the battle against a force that threatens to consume them all.

Little did they know that the answers they sought were hidden within the pages of an ancient book, a book that would lead them on a perilous adventure through the shadows of St. Mary's School?

Introduction

In the misty hills of Shimla, nestled at the peak of a mountain, stood the mysterious St. Mary School hidden deep within dense forests. While the school appeared ordinary to

 outsiders, the locals whispered of its dark secrets. Tales of students disappearin g without a trace and ghostly apparitions roaming its corridors were rampant. The most chilling rumor was of a curse that bound the townsfolk to silence, forbidding them from revealing the school's mysteries to outsiders. Those who dared to speak of its secrets faced dire consequences, adding to the school's aura of fear and intrigue. As a result, St. Mary

remained a haunting enigma, a place where
the line between reality and legend blurred,
drawing only the bravest to seek
its hidden truths.

This led to only outsiders enrolling their
children at St. Mary, and they were never able
to reach them again.

*"It remained a mystery where children went
missing. It was purportedly the oldest school
nestled in the misty hills of Shimla. However,
scepticism persisted among some, prompting
numerous questions: Were these rumours true
or false? If true, where were the children
disappearing to?"*

Chapter-1

It was the first day at Daisy, Aarya, Aayaan, Trisha, and Roy's new school. Their parents had enrolled them midway through the academic year as lateral entries. Upon arriving that morning, everything seemed normal with other children visible at the boarding school. Despite the hostel's mixed condition of cleanliness, the five of them found solace in each other's company amidst initial disappointment. They quickly formed a pact to support one another from day one, ensuring their rooms were among the neatest in the hostel.

As they settled in, things appeared normal until Aayaan heard an odd noise from the ground while playing, though he dismissed it. Later, at dinner in the mess hall, they were surprised not to see any other children around. They brushed it off, assuming the others were simply running late.

The night attendance was odd. The teachers, Anmol and Purnima, seemed unusual while checking roll call. The five students were all assigned to the same room, so they were sleeping together. Roy felt something strange while trying to sleep but didn't say anything since everyone else was asleep.

For nearly a month, the students felt uneasy at school. They had no way to contact their parents, as teachers did not allow them to use their mobile phones. Daisy, in particular, was deeply attached to her family and often cried. Despite these challenges, the five of them remained close friends, always supporting and never insulting one another.

In their classes, they rarely encountered other students, and if they did, they would quickly disappear. They had seen only three to five teachers, who taught in a manner that made the material difficult to understand. The lack of engaging activities and extracurricular left them bored. With their parents unable to visit

and no way to return home, Daisy's
unhappiness motivated them to take action.

Chapter-2

Nearly a month had passed, and their patience had worn thin. They resolved to escape from school, choosing Thursday for their daring plan. That night, at precisely 12:30 a.m., they attempted their escape, confident that they would remain undetected. However, reality proved otherwise.

As they stepped out through the gate, an

unsettling sense of dread overcame them. It felt as though someone was trailing behind. The sound of footsteps multiplied, growing louder and more numerous. With trembling resolve, they turned around and were met with an astonishing sight: a vast throng of ghostly children's souls pursuing them. The sight was so terrifying that Trisha fainted. They carried her and fled in panic.

Along the way, they too eventually succumbed to unconsciousness. When they awoke the next morning, they found themselves in their school's hostel, lying in their beds. On the table beside them was a peculiar joker card. Despite its presence, the real sense of foreboding came from the room next door, which remains eerily empty and where no one who entered was never seen again.

As they went to school for classes, as usual no one was there except those teachers. Today their school's Principal came to their class, whose name was Joseph. He was looking dangerous; his teeth were yellowish, white and grey hairs, dry lips of brown colour. He was with a totally a different face. His voice was so hoarse. They five were so frightened of him. Joseph asked them question, but thankfully they knew answers of all the questions asked to them. The Principal went back to his office and the students got relief. However, they were thinking about the last night's scene. Also, today was their library's period. They went to library, but it was broken and having spider's net, torn and all the books were so old and with a layer of dust on their covers. After watching that, all their interest of reading books flew away. However, it was too difficult to spend the forty minutes in that library with that dangerous librarian, Henry… He was also looking similar to their school's Principal.

Chapter-3

One day, while they were wandering in the corridors they saw Henry going to a room next to library, which was never seen before by them. In addition to, they saw Henry going to that room first time and while roaming they

went closer to library but couldn't find any room there. Library was locked but sound of hitting something and different strange sounds were coming from inside. They got afraid to those sounds and ran away. After, in class, they also thought that this was their misunderstanding and ignored once, but, from that day they saw Henry going in that room continuously for one-two weeks and whenever they passes through the library different sounds were heard by them. They were having a fear from Henry and that invisible room. At the other hand, their parents couldn't reach them. After their admissions, they also heard about those rumours and were thinking that might be the rumours were true, were feeling bad and their mothers were about to cry.

They wanted to go and find that room but didn't have any idea for getting inside that room and to find it. At night they slept at 2:30 AM and were thinking about the room and of an idea to get inside.

However, after thinking a lot also, they didn't get any idea regarding that and also they were late to sleep and then slept. For the couple of weeks they kept thinking but didn't get any idea. Now, they had stopped thinking because their exams were coming closer and closer, approximately 15 days to go. Their all focus was on their exams and weren't able to see anything else.

On 7th February, their exams were started and were ended on 22nd February. Their exams went well but the question papers and their answer sheets were torn very badly, dusty and were printed on recycled paper, looking very old.

They were told that the result would be on 1ˢᵗ March. Till then, everything was going well, but, the new admissions, they five felt very strange when parents weren't invited even in the result, toppers weren't announced and even some of the students didn't receive the report cards also. Between these long periods of time, they had forgotten about that room, next to library whose secret they wanted to reveal.

Their new session was beginning from 5ᵗʰ March and the same day they saw Henry going again to that room. This time they also saw a strange thing, Joseph was with him. Then, they realised that something was going wrong or something else.

The same night, they made a plan and decided to work according to that. It was Monday and their library's period was on Friday. Their eyes were always on him, observing every movement.

Friday was coming closer and closer and it was then Wednesday, till then also everything was going well, but they didn't knew that when everything and their each thought would flip. Henry was behaving in a strange manner as he knew each and every thought coming in

their mind. They five also felt strange and
behaved normal. It was then Thursday and as
they knew what they have to do the next day,
they slept early that night with a hope for next
day.

Chapter-4

Friday had come; they were nervous yet curious about the room. They had many thoughts in their mind with many questions along with. The secret of the room may turn their journey into an adventure. In addition to this, anything could happen with them at any time, due to which, they had to be ready for every moment. They had decided to enter that

room during their library period and also no teacher would be in school till Sunday except their matron. Fourth period at 10:20 A.M. was of library. When they moved towards library with their class, a biggest scam happened with them; library was locked and Henry wasn't in the whole school campus. Their whole expectations were flowed with water and they were like, they were never be able to enter the room, but now, Aayan the weakest among them gave them sympathy and made their thoughts positive and more strong to win.

They were now more prepared for their adventure, packed all the items they would need. Due to that scam, they changed their idea a bit and decided to enter the room when Henry would. For this, they had to wait Henry to come and enter the room which could take long for them as they had to also wait for Henry to reach school first and enter the room and the way they would be able to enter the room was more difficult for them. They had to wait outside, hiding behind something, for the whole school time and were arranging something to keep on their seats. They wanted a structure of body whose shape would look real. Now, they were waiting for Monday. They had arranged school dress and balloons for the shape of head and some other material for their body shape. This time all were ready with a new energy. Sunday's night was full of curiosity for them. They also didn't knew either they would be succeeded or have to face failure again, nothing was with a surety. Their heads were also in a whirl. They all slept after saying "all the best" to each other.

Good night...

Chapter-5

A morning with a shine and hope in their eyes of winning something was present. They had put the body structures on their benches in the way such that no one could identify it. They went behind the pillars near the library, and started waiting for Henry. There was no idea, when he would come. It was 11 AM, they were bored and were feeling sleepy, a strange sound like breaking of glass came and their eyes opened widely. They had become aware. Sound of steps was coming from behind, Trisha turned back, and it was Henry with something in his hand. They all escaped near library's door behind the large flower pots, where he wouldn't be able to see them.

Henry saw all around him and thought that there was no one around him, but he was wrong. He tapped at the small mark on the wall and the door appeared said the pin-code, "7112009", they have to quickly move inside the room behind Henry, as he moved inside he forgot to lock the door from key and it remained open, they all entered the room which was titled, "The Hidden Room of their School".

It might be their luck that the door remained open. As they looked around, it was an amazing room, full of books of different variety they had never seen before. However, they couldn't found Henry around. They were roaming around and thought that they were safe, but, didn't knew how Roy pressed a button near a book and all of them fell downwards through a slide where all things were black around and they couldn't see anything. When they reached the floor connected to the slide, they fell down and they all got fainted. Suddenly, Daisy's eyes opened and she saw Henry in front of her. She was so

frightened of her and quickly sat down and the strange thing was no other was there. She asked with a fear in a shrill voice, "W-W-W Where is my friends?"

Henry didn't said anything and

removed his fake skin of his face, which he used to wear during school time, which looks just like real and nobody could guess that it would be fake. In reality, Henry was so handsome and after seeing that Daisy's notions totally changed for him. Now, she wasn't afraid of him. Then, Henry replied her with a clear voice, "They all are on beds and sleeping well... But... how did you come to know about this room and how and when did you entered?" Daisy, sitting on the floor, told the entire scenario to Henry.

They also moved towards the room present there, where Aayan, Trisha, Roy and Aarya were sleeping. Daisy woke all of them up and they were surprised to see the man with her standing behind her. When they came to know that it was Henry, they all were surprised to hear that. While they were there in the bedroom talking, Henry told them that Joseph was also wearing a fake face mask.

However, after watching, they realized that it might be true and started trusting him. Joseph also entered and their conversation lasted for half an hour. In the evening, when it was time to leave, students were wandering here and there, Joseph and Henry left forgot about them and returned back to their homes. They were inside and realised when it was too much late there was no advantage of hitting the door even. Having no other choice, started roaming again. They were hungry and suffered for 2-3 days. Joseph had played that trick and they came to know about that from the clues in the room. According to them, Henry was good but had a doubt on Joseph.

Chapter-6

Henry visited there after three days. When he realized that those five remained there, various thoughts were coming in his mind. Anyway, when he reached to them, they seemed to be partially dead, lying on the bed. He gave them food to eat and water to drink and after having their meal they were looking fit and fine. They asked Henry that what they would do then, they were missing their parents and hadn't met them for a long period of time. Henry was good but didn't tell the secret of the school as all the teachers had took that pledge when they joined the school. That day, they all went together with Henry but while going back, passing through the racks of library Trisha saw a big and thick book with dusty brown cover, seemed to be old and was titled, *THE HIDDEN SECRET*. The book was looking different from other books. When they reached their room, Trisha was still thinking about that book and due to her curiosity she told about that to her friends. Obviously, after listening about that book they all also became curious about it and planned to visit there again. Now, Henry's behavior with them was good but Joseph didn't want to take them all again to that room and they came to know about it when they heard conversation between Joseph and David, their Vice Principal who used to come rarely. Joseph sticks to him so much as he also does job outside and knew much about the campus than him.

Henry was unaware of his thoughts until that moment. He didn't knew that Joseph was selfish and wanted to achieve something great without any hard work, just wanted to be supreme among all. He wasn't happy to be a principal, wanted the same book that Trisha wanted. The difference was that Trisha loved the book's appearance whereas Joseph wanted to know the secret hidden inside the book.

From that day, they again started to plan to reach there once again. The centre of attraction to visit there was that book. Students weren't aware of Joseph's planning; they were just trying their best. One day when they were approaching with Henry, Joseph interfered between them and it wasn't first time, it had happened many times with them, had noticed also but never reacted to him and took normally.

It was 23 May; they were going to ask Henry for visiting library and that book. As they spoke about the book, Joseph heard and was now dead sure that they wanted the book.

Joseph urged and went to Henry as early as they five left. He said to Henry that he was in a hurry and wanted to go in the room to find some books. Henry was feeling strange but gave him the door key to unlock the room. He quickly ran to the room and started to find the book but couldn't find it. On the other

hand, the five students saw the room open and went inside because Henry had not argued against them visiting the room. They were at the opposite sides, and didn't expect that they were finding the same book.

Unfortunately, Joseph found the book and kept in the bedroom's almirah. They weren't aware about it and randomly went to bedroom after some time, Daisy advised to look for it in bedroom also but all others refused. They tried all the day to find it but couldn't find it.

As usual they went to room and saw Joseph in bedroom, searching for something in an almirah. They were thinking to go inside but didn't and looked from outside the room and looked inside, hiding behind the book racks. He was continuously finding that book as someone had took it. Although, they didn't knew about it. He took so much time that they got bored, but just as they were about to leave, he found the book and became happier.

Many days spent like this only. Before they could solve one issue, they were already facing other problems along the way. Joseph had started to read that book and knew more about the school; the hidden ways, secrets of school, some secret rooms in which things like black magic were performed and some souls were still wandering there, ways to bring more students in school and how to hypnotise them or bring them under their control and many others. He was becoming horrible day by day. One day he was wearing torn up pants, shabby blazer with a pale coloured shirt inside it with sleepers at the bottom. All found him strange, but didn't know the reason behind his strange behaviour.

The book was playing a bad role for school, which may lead a haunted conclusion.

Chapter-7

All was going different in school. At the other side, they wanted to find that book, but what to do they didn't knew anything about the book's location. Book was actually having two parts inside it; Part A and Part B.

Joseph wanted to read only its Part B, which was the negative part of the book and all he wanted was in it.

It was Sunday's evening, Joseph wasn't in school and he forgot that book to carry with him and was kept on his office's table. Fortunately, they five didn't knew that he wasn't in the school that day and because Principal's office was open, they went inside, shocked to see the book and took it along with them and succeeded to take it to their room without getting in any one's eye. They went in the room back opened the book with a positive hope excitedly. The context page was having two parts as told before. Obviously, they wanted Part A. They first flipped through all the pages swiftly, then opened to the first page and started to read it thoroughly. It was positive so it had positive aspects of school and also later they found cures of the negatively spreading in their school sue to Joseph. The various methods, activities were given to heal those negative vibes.

The book was hidden beyond the reach of Joseph in their room and didn't take it out of their room.

Joseph's powers were getting weak day by day. He wasn't able to find the thief of the book who stole it. He was trying so much to find it, but couldn't. He had also forgotten about those five but once he saw them again, got a doubt of stealing on them.

He tried to stock them many times but couldn't because they got some powers after reading that book and suddenly got disappeared.

Nothing could happen and the book remained with them. With time, the school was having positive aspects.

Chapter-8

It was the time now, when the positive part of the book was at the end and three to four pages were left, nothing special except the second last and last page.

In the second last page, it was for reading the directions and in the last page, the most important or we can say it a magical page.

When they opened that page and followed the directions. It had a picture of school which was totally different from their school. In directions, they were given three questions to find, which were related to their school campus, but didn't knew the result. (Hint was given with each) along with a common hint.

First question- *Who is your real school Principal?*

Hint- *You need to search him may be in the dark places of school or secret places; may found some hints in Part A.*

Second question- *What was the main aim of Joseph?*

Hint- *You may know about it before or you may get a doubt earlier about it.*

Third question- *Whose secret room was that and how Henry became its owner?*

Hint- *You may saw him earlier when you came but not again, may come to know about it your old Principal.*

Common hint*- May find it at one place, which is dark but full of colors.*

They were surprised to see these questions and were completely confused. It was strange to hear the first question about their Principal. As much they knew about Principal he was, Joseph. They wrote Joseph in the blank provided to fill the answer. They were having a strange reaction and were shocked to see that it was incorrect answer and as a result, Joseph wasn't their principal.

Now they had to find the real Principal of their school, a person they neither knew nor had seen him ever. They decided to search for him from next morning. Firstly, they went to Henry and asked him indirectly about Principal by saying, "Who was the Principal here before Joseph, or he is the first?" Henry's face was looking pale but hiding his expression said, "I don't know because when I came here, Joseph was Principal of this school and I didn't ask anything about it from anyone." After taking a break he said, "Why you want to know about it?" They said without thinking anything, "We were writing a paragraph on school's history." "Ok, Ok", Henry said.

They went from there discussing their plans. Then, they went to the dark places of school, in store, where all the things were old and full of dust with no lights. In the back court's sports room where no one goes, in the room where no one lives, but didn't find anything. They were also curious to know about him, but unable to find him. They found him everywhere but couldn't. Next day, they went to the library's secret room without informing Henry, it was Roy's idea and may work. They locked the room from inside. They went to bedroom while wandering, while they were inside bedroom, Aayan was looking at the books arranged badly in the bookshelves. He started to arrange them and found an old, rusty lever in the bookshelf. He shouted and called his friend to show them the lever. All came there and decided to pull it up. Roy tried to pull it but it was too hard and rusty, which made him difficult to pull it.

They all tried together to pull it and after

applying much force it shifted slowly and after sometime it was pulled up completely. It was pulled up completely, a sound came like an old, rusty door was opened after a long time. The sound was coming from bedroom. They rushed to the room, and dust could be seen coming from under the bed. They quickly shifted the bed and found an underground door, which was filled with darkness and covered in dust. They had no surety that it would be safe or not. They kept the bed back to its place and went back to their room. Now they were just thinking about the hidden door, their Principal, Joseph and Henry.

Chapter-9

They went back and locked the door from the inside. Slowly, they shifted the bed and prepared themselves to enter the room. They turned on their flashlights and stepped inside, only to find it was like a slide, causing them all to slip down to the end. There, they found eight tunnels to move forward. The tunnels had signboards, but they were rusted and partially broken, making them illegible.

They decided to enter one of the tunnels, counting the fifth one from their front. Before proceeding, they left an empty red Lays wrapper as a marker, indicating where they had started.

As they entered the tunnel, it grew darker. Suddenly, they saw a beam of light coming from a small hole in the wall. As they kept moving, that beam of light expanded, looking like they were standing in front of a cream-colored LED cinema screen. The light's high reflection caused them all to faint, and then the light disappeared, leaving the tunnel dark again.

After some time, a drop of water fell on Aarya's forehead, waking her up. She couldn't see anything around, as their flashlights had turned off due to worn-out batteries. She quickly took out extra batteries from her bag and turned the flashlight back on. She woke up the others and they decided to move more carefully.

As they moved forward, they kept ending up at the same place instead of finding something new. This happened one, two, three, four, five times. On the sixth attempt, they decided to go back but realized they didn't know the way home. They chose to enter another tunnel, tunnel number three, in hopes of reaching somewhere, even if it wasn't back to their hostel.

But this time, instead of ending up in the same place, they discovered a door. Filled with hope, they believed they were close to their first goal of finding their Principal. As they approached the door, they noticed it was old, with a thick layer of dust and rust underneath. The dust was so thick that a finger could easily sink into it. They tried to open the door, but it didn't even budge.

While Daisy explored the area, which looked like an open room, the others were trying to figure out how to open the door. As Daisy walked around, she accidentally stepped on a tile that pressed down like an enter button on a computer. Suddenly, the dust on the door scattered, and it began to vibrate like a huge bulldozer. However, it didn't open and soon stopped vibrating, returning to normal.

Then they noticed a keyhole in the door with a small rolled-up piece of paper inside it. They carefully took out the paper and unrolled it. Although the text wasn't very clear, they managed to read the message: 'I know your goal in coming here, which is just on the other side of this door. But to achieve it, you have to insert the correct key into this keyhole and open it. All your answers are waiting for you.'

After reading this, they felt their goal was within reach and believed they would find at least one answer there. However, their next

challenge was finding the right key to open the
door.

Chapter-10

They stayed there and thought about it but had no idea but were sure that it would be around their only. They also left a packet there and went back to the place from where they started and entered the tunnel number eight, because they had only not went in that tunnel and there, they found a box which looks like a treasure box. It had no lock but was made of iron and covered with rust on it and was too much heavy that it wasn't possible to open it alone for them. They were meticulously searching every nook and cranny of the room for the elusive key. Suddenly, Trisha felt a strange pull on her wrist. A magnet had been attracted to the metal bracelet she was wearing and was now firmly attached to it. Curiosity piqued, she moved the magnet closer to the treasure box, and to everyone's amazement, the box started to vibrate gently. Intrigued, she pulled the magnet away, and the vibration ceased immediately.

This peculiar occurrence sparked an idea in Roy's mind. He suggested that they should try bringing the magnet near the treasure box again to see what might happen. As Trisha brought the magnet closer to the box once more, a bright light suddenly emanated from it, illuminating the room for a few seconds before disappearing as quickly as it had appeared.

The magnet remained stuck to Trisha's bracelet, and the group exchanged bewildered glances. With a sense of anticipation, Aayan

reached out and, to everyone's surprise, the treasure box opened effortlessly. Inside, they found an array of mysterious objects and ancient artefacts, hinting at secrets long forgotten and adventures yet to be unravelled.

The key was kept inside the glass box and they took it out and moved towards door.

As they reached back to the place from where they had started, they entered tunnel number two instead of tunnel number three. Yet this time they didn't return to the same spot but found a gate similar to the previous one. They put the key in the hole, and it opened. The room had a foul smell, old skeletons, and many other weird things. As they turned back to the door, they found it closed. When they knocked on it, they felt a reverse force on their bodies.

Then they saw five empty chairs and understood that they were meant for their skeletons. It didn't stop there; they saw a soul in front of them knocking on the door just like they had been doing earlier. They realized it was the soul of a child, part of a group of souls of children who had tried to run away from school. They searched for the key they had found in the treasure box, as it had fallen between the skeletons due to magic tricks performed by the souls inside. After much struggle, they found the key; put it back in the keyhole, and the door opened. They ran outside the room, pulled the key out, and went into the correct tunnel this time.

Chapter-11

As they reached their destination, their happiness knew no bounds. The anticipation of being so close to their goal filled them with renewed energy. With a sense of excitement, they carefully inserted the key into the keyhole. Immediately, a bright light radiated from the hole, illuminating their faces, and the door swung open effortlessly, as if welcoming them.

Stepping into the room, they were immediately struck by the oppressive heat and the suffocating presence of carbon dioxide and other poisonous gases. The air was thick and heavy, making it hard to breathe. Daisy, unable to withstand the harsh environment, fainted almost instantly.

The room's temperature was unbearably high, and they could feel the sweat pouring down their faces and backs. Despite the discomfort, the four remaining friends knew they had to stay strong and find a way to survive. They supported each other, taking turns to check on Daisy while fanning her and trying to cool her down.

Minutes felt like hours as they struggled to breathe and adapt to the harsh conditions. Eventually, the air quality began to improve, and the room's temperature slowly returned to a more bearable level. They breathed a collective sigh of relief, finally able to take in fresh breaths. Their immediate concern was Daisy, who was still unconscious. They tended to her with care, hoping she would regain consciousness soon.

The ordeal had brought them even closer together, reinforcing their determination to see their quest through to the end. As they gathered their strength and composure, they couldn't help but feel a mix of relief and apprehension about what lay ahead. The challenges they had faced so far had been daunting, but they knew they had to persevere, for the sake of their goal and each other.

In the room, they discovered an old wooden almirah. The almirah had no lock or any other mechanism to prevent them from opening it, and its door was already slightly ajar. Curiosity piqued, they approached and pulled the door open. Inside, the shelves were filled with numerous books, each covered in a thick layer of dust. The books looked old and neglected, their pages yellowed with age and

their covers worn and tattered.

As they scanned the collection, they noticed something unusual. Amidst the dusty and worn volumes, one book stood out. It was not only neat and clean but also seemed to radiate a peculiar glow. Unlike the others, its cover shone with a strange luminescence that made it appear almost otherworldly. The contrast between this book and the rest of the collection was striking, drawing their attention immediately.

Their excitement grew as they reached for the glowing book, eager to uncover the secrets it held. The discovery of this unique book amidst the otherwise ordinary collection hinted at hidden mysteries and adventures waiting to be explored.

Aayan picked up the book and realized it was the third part of the series, or rather, the second book. On the first page, it was written about the 'Hidden Secret; Part A and Part B, Joseph's Introduction and Henry's Intro.' The main concept was revealed in the note, which read, 'The previous part of the book was written by Principal Sir, and this book is by me, his wife. You might think its Joseph, but it is not. This book was written by the Principal before him, the one you have been seeking and have now found because you possess the first part of this book.'

They were surprised by this revelation. It was a kind of magical book with mysterious powers that made it difficult to open. The pages wouldn't even turn easily, as it required some special tricks to unlock its secrets.

The twelve pages were difficult to open and read, and they mentioned the Principal's wife, Stuti. At the bottom of the twelfth page, it was stated that the fifteenth page would be about the Principal. However, opening the next page required significant power or high-order thinking skills. When they learned about the requirement for such a mind, they thought of Daisy, who unfortunately was not awake. They also did not have any water to sprinkle on her face to revive her. Aayan wandered around the room in search of water and discovered a small iron window. He pulled it open with effort and saw water inside. He shouted in excitement, "See guys, water!"

The group was both confused and happy to see water flowing there. Aayan took some water in his hand and tried to bring it to Daisy, but the water accidentally spilled over the book near her. The twelfth page got wet, causing their heartbeats to quicken. Aayan quickly picked up the book and moved the water aside, while Trisha sprinkled some water on Daisy's face. Daisy opened her eyes and sat up suddenly. They told her about the book and asked if she could try to open the next page with her super mind, as she often thought fast and effectively.

Daisy took the book and tried to turn the page normally, and to their amazement, the page turned easily. However, the following page was again difficult to open. Daisy asked if anything unusual had been done to the previous page. Roy suddenly recalled, "Yes, remember the water was sprinkled on the page. Let's try it once more. Maybe that's the key. They filled their empty bottles with the water, while Daisy placed the mysterious book under the flowing water. Surprisingly, the book didn't get wet, and the pages began to turn like those of a normal book. As they flipped through the previous pages, they discovered information about another secret room, linked to Henry's secret room. However, they were unable to explore it at that moment and decided to ignore it for now.

Upon reaching the fifteenth page, they found detailed information about the Principal. The page included the Principal's name, date of birth, date of death, and other significant details. The revelations left them both intrigued and uneasy, as they began to piece together the story behind the Principal's life and the hidden secrets of the school.

The page was centre-aligned and titled "Our Principal" in bold, bloody red letters, written in a strange, ominous font. Beneath the title was a photograph of the Principal, accompanied by every detail about him. They meticulously read each word with intense scrutiny.

His name was Mr Edward. Upon reading his name, Aarya felt a jolt of recognition. She examined his photograph with heightened focus. Suddenly, she exclaimed, "Didn't you see this same picture in Henry's secret room, above his table in the bedroom?"

Her revelation sent a wave of realization through the group, connecting the Principal to the mysterious and hidden aspects of Henry's secret room. The plot thickened, and they knew they were on the verge of uncovering deeper secrets that tied their discoveries together.

One by one, they all remembered seeing the photograph in Henry's secret room. As they continued reading the entire page, they felt a sense of growing unease. With trepidation, they turned to the next page, and their hearts skipped a beat as they read the ominous message:

"If you have read the full page of Our Principal, be aware he is behind you, waiting for

you to turn back."

A cold shiver ran down their spines. The room seemed to grow darker and more oppressive. They instinctively huddled closer together, their eyes darting around the room, too afraid to turn and look behind them. The silence was deafening, filled only by the sound of their rapid breathing and pounding hearts. Each of them knew that whatever happened next, they would face it together, hoping that their unity and courage would see them through the unknown terror that lay in wait.

Aayan, sensing the mounting fear, urged everyone to stay calm. He requested the bottle in which they had stored the water from the mysterious window. With steady hands, he opened the bottle and cupped some water in his palm, believing that only this water held the power to dispel the Principal's soul. He instructed everyone to turn around. As the shadow of the Principal's soul loomed before them, Aayan flung the water at it with determination. The moment the water made contact, the shadow scattered into the air, dissolving into nothingness.

With the immediate threat gone, they exhaled a collective sigh of relief. The experience had reaffirmed their belief in the book's ominous truths. Each word written in its pages held a weight and reality they could no longer deny.

Chapter-12

Having decided to take the book back to their hostel, they suddenly realized they didn't know the way back. A wave of confusion and apprehension swept over the group. Aayan, after a moment of thought, shrugged his shoulders and said with a sudden jerk, "Maybe we find the solution in the book itself."

"Yes, it may work," Daisy replied, hope lighting up her eyes.

They began reading the pages backward from the fifteenth, each turn of the page a step closer to potential salvation. To their surprise, they found the solution on the very same page.

It was a detailed, albeit cryptic, set of instructions.

Despite the danger it seemed to imply, they decided to

implement the plan. With hearts pounding and nerves on edge, they followed the book's directions. Each step felt fraught with peril, but they moved forward with determination, trusting that the book, which had already guided them through so many challenges, would lead them back safely.

First, they went back to the area and then to tunnel number two, where they saw the gate they had opened earlier, which was previously filled with skeletons. Written on the gate was a message: "The gate will open and the souls inside have gone to heaven. They will no longer disturb us." As they moved slowly towards the gate, it opened on its own. They nudged the door with their feet. To their amazement, the area appeared much cleaner than before, and there were no skeletons in sight.

Their eyes scanned the room, taking in every object that was kept there. Among the various items, an almirah caught their attention. It seemed handmade, adorned with intricate and beautiful carvings that gave it an almost magical aura. The craftsmanship was exquisite, and they couldn't help but marvel at its beauty.

Curiosity piqued, they approached the almirah, wondering what secrets it might hold. The room once filled with dread and darkness, now felt like a place of hidden treasures and untold stories waiting to be discovered.

When they opened the almirah, it emitted a bright yellowish glitter that illuminated a path ahead. Written on the inside, they found a message: "Enter and proceed with caution, as any obstacle may arise in your way. This is the final step to reach your goal."

Gathering their courage, they stepped into the glowing pathway. As they moved forward, the light began to fade, plunging them into complete darkness. Eerie ghostly sounds echoed around them, heightening their fear.

Despite the spine-chilling atmosphere, they held each other's hands tightly, drawing strength from their unity. With a shared determination, they ran quickly through the darkness, their hearts pounding in their chests. This was the first obstacle in their journey, a test of their resolve and teamwork.

Every step forward felt like a challenge, but they knew that together, they could face whatever lay ahead.

The next obstacle emerged swiftly; many pebbles started falling on them like a torrential rain. The sharp, relentless shower made it difficult to see or move forward. Trisha, exhausted from the relentless pace, began to stumble. She was on the brink of fainting, her strength nearly gone.

Seeing her struggle, Aayan acted swiftly. He scooped her up in his arms, shielding her from the falling pebbles with his own body. With determination and courage, he ran, protecting both Trisha and himself from the onslaught. The others followed closely, supporting each other as they navigated through the barrage.

Their teamwork and resilience shone through as they pushed forward, determined to overcome whatever lay ahead.

The book had clearly stated that there would be five obstacles every twenty minutes. If they took even one extra minute, five more obstacles would appear. Seven minutes had already passed, leaving them with only thirteen minutes to navigate the remaining three obstacles.

With the countdown looming over them, the group knew they had to manage their time meticulously. They had successfully overcome the first two obstacles, but three were still left. The book warned that these final challenges would be the most difficult and would come simultaneously.

The tension in the air was palpable as they prepared for the impending trials. Each member of the group steeled themselves, knowing that their success depended on their unity and quick thinking. The clock was ticking, and the path ahead promised to test their limits in ways they had never imagined.

A thunderstorm erupted, accompanied by a tornado and heavy rainfall, creating a terrifying and haunted atmosphere. These elements alone were enough to frighten them, causing them to pull back in fear. As they navigated through the chaos, they encountered a girl standing in their path, crying. Drawn closer by her sobs, they were horrified to see her face transform into a menacing visage, reminiscent of when Munjya possessed Bela in the 2024 movie "Munjya."

Panic surged through them, and they fled the scene as quickly as they could. With only two minutes remaining, they knew that failing to reach the door in time would mean facing five even more formidable obstacles. Their desperation fuelled their speed, and they ran faster than ever before.

Through the blinding rain and fierce winds, they finally glimpsed a door connected to their hostel. It was their only hope of escape. They were thirty meters away with just twenty seconds left. Pushing their limits, they sprinted towards the door, each second ticking away like a countdown to their doom.

In a final burst of energy, they crossed the threshold with only 1.7 seconds to spare. Relief washed over them as they stepped onto the other side, knowing they had narrowly escaped a fate far worse than anything they had imagined.

As they turned around, the path behind them vanished, leaving them bewildered. When they looked ahead, they found themselves in a familiar yet unexpected place—the area behind their own room's almirah. To their astonishment, the almirah had moved on its own, creating a passage for them to step through.

Despite the wonder of this unexpected occurrence, they ignored the almirah and stepped forward, relieved to be back in a familiar setting. Little did they know the almirah held its own secrets, mysteries yet to be uncovered? As they caught their breath and glanced around, the room seemed to hold an air of anticipation, as if more revelations were waiting just around the corner.

Chapter-13

As they glanced at the clock, they noticed it was exactly 1:00 AM. Exhausted from their three-day ordeal, they decided it was best to get some rest. The fatigue weighed heavily on their eyelids as they drifted into slumber.

"In the dead of night, Daisy saw a light emanating from the almirah, accompanied by strange, eerie sounds. Without a second thought, she moved toward it, drawn by curiosity and an inexplicable pull. As she stepped through the almirah, she found herself in a strange room. Suddenly, she heard her name being called out repeatedly, "Daisy! Daisy! Daisy!"

She felt a minor earthquake, the ground trembling beneath her feet. Startled, she jolted awake, her heart racing. It took her a moment to realize that it was all just a dream—or perhaps, a nightmare. The vividness of the experience left her deeply unsettled.

The next morning, the group considered asking Henry about Mr Edward, but ultimately decided against it. Each person offered their own advice and theories, but Daisy remained preoccupied with her dream. The haunting experience lingered in her mind, casting a shadow over her thoughts.

Despite the lingering unease, they decided to go to school as usual and meet Henry, hoping that the answers they sought might be revealed in the light of day.

First, they went to their classrooms and immediately felt something was off. The usually cluttered and chaotic rooms were unexpectedly spotless. It was as if someone had meticulously cleaned and organized everything overnight. The stark contrast left them feeling both puzzled and uneasy.

Surprised by the pristine condition of the classrooms, they couldn't shake the feeling that something was amiss. With this strange occurrence lingering in their minds, they decided to head to Henry's secret room. They hoped that he might have some answers.

Upon entering the secret room, they found Henry there, waiting. His presence felt reassuring, but the mystery of the clean classrooms still loomed large in their thoughts.

Henry, with a perplexed expression, asked them, "Do you know who closed the door from the inside when no one was in the room?" The children exchanged puzzled glances, each uncertain of the answer.

Gathering their thoughts, they began recounting all the strange events they had experienced. As they spoke, Henry listened intently, his face growing more serious with each detail they revealed.

When he realized that the children knew about Mr Edward, his reaction was one of shock. He stood speechless, grappling with the weight of their discovery. The revelation seemed to pierce through the veil of mystery that had shrouded their journey, leaving them all in a profound silence.

After that, they showed Henry both books—*The Hidden Secret* and its sequel. Henry was familiar only with the first book, authored by Mr Edward. He himself was unaware of some of the deeper secrets contained within. As he leafed through the pages, his eyes welled up with tears, which soon spilled over, rolling down his cheeks. He sobbed uncontrollably, leaving the children puzzled and concerned.

Fearful yet determined, Daisy stepped forward gently placing her hand on Henry's forehead, she asked with a trembling voice, "What... what happened to you? Why are you crying?"

Through his tears, Henry replied, "I can see flashbacks of my life."

His words hung in the air, heavy with the weight of past memories and unresolved mysteries. The children sensed that the books held more significance than they had initially realized, and that Henry's emotional reaction was a key to unlocking the deeper truths they sought.

"Flash back? What kind of flashbacks?" Daisy asked with concern.

"Mr Edward..." Henry began.

"You know him... how?" Roy asked his curiosity piqued.

"He is... my..." Henry stammered.

"Who, what's your relation with him? Please tell us," Trisha urged.

"My… my… my father. He is my father," Henry finally confessed.

"Your father?" they all shouted in unison, their voices echoing through the room.

"Yes, he's my father," Henry confirmed.

"It means your mother is…" Aayan began.

"Stuti, yes she is my mother," Henry acknowledged.

"Then why didn't you tell us this before?" Daisy asked, trying to understand.

"I didn't want to remind myself of the past again," Henry replied, his voice heavy with emotion.

"Okay, don't worry," Daisy said reassuringly. "But can you help us now to reach them?"

There were many secrets hidden within the text, encrypted in difficult code words. Without an expert, they turned to Henry, who found a book written by a renowned cryptographer in the library's almirah.

After several hours of painstaking work, they successfully translated the cryptic words into English. The message they uncovered was:

"The beginning and conclusion are written in the books only. The words are just provided for a hint; you have to delve deep into them to find the beginning. It is better if you can also conclude it as written."

Realizing the true secrets were embedded within the books, they understood they needed to analyse the text meticulously to uncover the hidden truths.

"Similarly, the room of heroes would be Room No. 105. They will come and spread peace all around. The school would be forgiven for every mistake and may become the best in the world once again. The room holds a secret. You know it but have ignored it. Remember the day you returned while bringing me back to school?"

Eager to continue, they found the codes ended abruptly. Disappointed but hopeful, they reminded themselves that everything happens for a reason. They revisited the phrase "Room No. 105" and realized something eerie. The room had been occupied until the day they arrived, but it was empty when they entered. The previous occupant had committed suicide in the boys' washroom on that very day.

Henry, sensing their dismay, motivated them. "You are those heroes, and you'll perform a miracle that will restore St. Mary to its former glory."

With renewed determination, they stood in a circle, placing their hands on top of each other's. They made a solemn vow, "We will all try until our school becomes the best in the world."

Chapter-14

They started searching for things that could help them in their quest. They discovered that the Principal's body was hidden somewhere, but only the killer knew its location. Henry revealed this, adding that the book might contain clues, and they should meticulously read every page.

"Yes, we should. Let's sprinkle some water that we got from that iron window," suggested Daisy.

They retrieved the water bottle and sprinkled water on the pages. As they read, they uncovered secrets even Henry hadn't known. He was astonished by these revelations. On the 25th page, they found information about the secrets of the almirah. Deciding to follow the instructions, they went to their room and carefully executed each step outlined in the book.

They took the almirah's key, opened it slowly, and removed all the items from inside. Knocking on its surface, a vibration was produced, revealing a hidden tunnel. Daisy suddenly remembered the nightmare she had the previous night and interrupted, "Don't go in there like this. It's a haunted and chilled place; you could turn into an ice cream. We need to read all the steps first and then follow them

because... I had a dream about this place, and it seemed very dangerous. There was a large, old box that kept moving away from me as I chased it. My dream broke when I fell while running after it."

Henry, feeling a mix of disbelief and caution, replied, "Okay, it means we should think it through before going in once more."

They sat in the hostel on their beds, and Henry motivated himself by recalling the scene of his father's death. He was determined to find the culprit who had killed his father and denied the family the chance to perform the necessary rituals. Henry was the only remaining descendant of his family. He also shared that when his father died, they found a note in his room that read, "Mr Edward has been killed, and his body is hidden in the darkest area where no one can reach except me until the right people come to give his soul peace."

They took out warm clothes, and Henry had some books that contained instructions for making useful items from small products. One of the books had a procedure for making a lotion that would keep them warm after applying it to their bodies. They were nervous yet curious about going there.

That night, Henry and the five children slept in the hostel together. While the others slept, Henry was still thinking about their mission. He heard a sound from outside their room's window. When he looked out, he saw something inconceivable happening downstairs. By the time he reached there, everything had disappeared. As he climbed the stairs back up, he heard a sound like someone shouting in the pain of death. When he returned to his bed, he lay down and thought about it for half the night, finally falling asleep at 4:30 a.m.

In the morning, Henry told the others about what he had seen. "When I looked out the window, I saw a lady killing a man wearing a black blazer and trousers. She was holding him from behind and trying to stab him in the back," he explained. He also mentioned the sounds he heard while coming upstairs.

The others suggested it might have been a dream, but Henry insisted it was real. After much discussion, the children agreed for Henry's self-satisfaction. They ate breakfast and prepared to move towards the hidden place they were curious about.

They took both books with them to find more evidence. They were so focused on finding the Principal's body that they had forgotten about the questions. When they opened the first book's page with the questions, they remembered their aim and goal. They filled in Mr Edward's name in the blank, which provided more hints for the second question: "You are moving on the right path, and the place you are going is close to Mr Edward's body. You can ask him questions that may help you."

They hadn't realized how helpful their room's almirah would be, with a secret door beyond their imagination.

They reached their destination after overcoming many obstacles. As they continued forward, the temperature kept dropping.

Thankfully, the cream they had made and applied to their bodies was effective, keeping them warm despite the cold. They also navigated through icebergs that fell diagonally from the walls, passing through with some difficulty but without major mishaps.

The room matched Daisy's description exactly. They moved forward and were soon engulfed in complete darkness. The pitch-black

surroundings made it impossible to see anything. Hoping to find a torch in their bags, they started searching through their belongings in the darkness. Fortunately, Trisha found a torch in her bag. When she took it out and turned it on, they saw...

Chapter-15

The sight before them was entirely unexpected. They huddled together, shivering as if surrounded by snow. Their eyes widened in astonishment as they beheld a massive door, towering as high as a ten-story building. The door was adorned with intricate carvings, which gave it a haunted appearance. Skeletons of humans and animals surrounded them, adding to the eerie atmosphere. Bats fluttered above their heads as they directed their torch towards the ceiling.

Though scared, they didn't lose heart. They remembered the codes written in the book and noticed that the carvings on the door matched those symbols. By sheer luck, Aayan had packed the book of codes in his bag, which helped them decipher the meanings. The message they received read: "Open the door to find your goal; the soul you seek might be here. Half of your targets lie behind me. Don't forget to pull the lever; it may be under you. Always remember, the codes in the book you found in the almirah may link back to the almirah from which you arrived."

They were astonished to find that everything they had read in the book was happening in real life, as if the book had been written in real-time. Every detail was perfectly aligned with their experiences and future encounters.

They delved into the words and concluded they needed to find another lever, which was hidden underground. To uncover it, they had to locate a specific block in the wall that, when pushed, would reveal the lever. Determined, they began their search. The students scoured the walls while Henry focused on the book. As everyone was immersed in their task, Henry suddenly shouted, "Oh, I got it!"

They all turned back and exclaimed in unison, "What? What did you find?"

"The block we're looking for is written to be higher than our reach. We need to get to a height of about thirty-two feet," Henry read aloud. "Unfortunately, we can't reach that high even if we stand on each other's shoulders. Our total height would be at most thirty-one feet."

They now knew which wall the block was on, but the height presented a significant challenge. After searching extensively for anything that could help them reaches that height, they came up empty-handed.

At last, Daisy recalled that the room resembled the one in her dream. "Wait, I almost forgot to mention—I saw a large box in my dream that kept moving away as I chased it," she said.

"But what's the role of that box here?" Roy asked, making a puzzled face.

"Yes, it will help us. We must find it, it was..." Daisy started to say, but Aarya interrupted, "Look, I found something really large over here!"

They all turned around and saw a dusty, old, and enormous box in the corner. As they moved closer, they felt an opposing force pushing them back. Forming a semicircle around the box, they tried to move towards it, but to no avail.

Aayan had a clever idea. Remembering the magnet they had used to open a previous box, he pointed it at the large box. To their relief, the magnet attracted the box, pulling it closer. The opposing force between them and the box vanished, allowing Roy to approach it.

They all stepped forward with a jerk. They realized that by placing the box at the bottom, they could reach the height needed to press the correct block. With anticipation, they climbed the box and pressed the block, revealing the lever.

The door vibrated loudly, shaking off rust and sending dust flying like a desert storm. It opened with a grating sound, like old iron being rubbed together after years. As the door swung open, their eyes shone brightly, like a pole star in a moonless night.

When the door fully opened, an old handwritten note fell onto Aarya's face with a strong gust. She snatched it from her face and read aloud, "Welcome. Here you will get all your answers... but only if you do it perfectly."

They were overjoyed, knowing they were close to their goal, the reason they had taken admission for this journey.

Chapter-16

They cautiously moved inside and saw a casket with Mr Edward's name spelled out in wooden blocks. That moment of realization sent chills down their spines as they comprehended that Mr Edward's corpse was inside the casket.

 They understood what lay within, but the thought of opening the casket filled them with fear. Henry, being his son, had not seen his father during his last moments. Without thinking, he opened the casket. Inside, his father's body lay peacefully, and upon seeing him, tears streamed down Henry's cheeks. The lack of rituals following his father's death

made the moment even more poignant. Suddenly, his father's soul emerged from the casket and appeared before them. The sight of the apparition filled everyone with fear, but Henry's longing to embrace his father overcame his fear.

The soul spoke emotionally, "Henry, my son, you are still alive."

Henry's voice trembled with emotion as he replied, "Yes, I am fine and here in front of you, Father."

"I knew you would come to me someday," his father's spirit said with a bittersweet smile, his spectral form flickering gently. Noticing the five children, he added with curiosity, "Are these... or what..."

Henry's eyes filled with unshed tears as he responded, "No, I haven't married since you and Mom passed away. These are school students who helped me reach you."

"Oh, hi, little champs!" his father's spirit greeted warmly. The children's eyes widened and they stood shivering, unsure of how to respond. An uncomfortable silence lingered, stretching on for what felt like an eternity.

Finally, Aarya found the courage to break the silence, "Hi, Good... Namaste." She was unsure of what to say, so she offered a respectful greeting, her voice barely above a whisper.

The atmosphere was charged with a mix of fear, relief, and the deep longing of a son reunited with his father's spirit. Each of them felt the weight of the moment, a blend of the supernatural and the profound emotions tied to lose loved ones.

"Don't be scared of me. I am your old Principal," Edward's soul spoke gently, trying to calm the children.

Henry stepped forward, "Dad, they're here for a reason."

"Tell me, what do you champs want?" Edward inquired with genuine curiosity.

"Actually, we don't want anything except some answers," Daisy replied, her voice steady. "Answers that will help us make our school the best in the world."

Edward's expression shifted as a doubt crossed his mind. *"Are you talking about...THE HIDDEN SECRET?"*

They all exchanged glances, a wave of realization washing over them. It dawned on them that the book was written by him. "Oh, yes! We forgot that you wrote the book," Henry said, the realization hitting him like a bolt. "If you wrote it, you must know the answers as well."

"Yes, I should, but I didn't know all the answers properly because the questions were written by one of my colleagues," Edward explained. "He was a kind of astrologer, someone who could easily predict the future. When he wrote the questions, he told me they would help me someday. Today, I see he was right. I'm so thankful to him, and it would be wonderful to meet him again, but that's impossible now... Anyway, let's move on. Could you show me those questions once more?"

They handed the book to Edward, who began to examine the questions closely.

Edward read through the questions and saw his name in the first one. Realizing he hadn't mentioned his name anywhere in the book, he asked, "Who told you my name?"

The students explained the scenarios that led them to his name.

When they showed him Stuti's book, Edward's expression darkened. "She copied the same name from my book," he said angrily. "She wrote it without telling me and declared it the second part."

The students were shocked by his reaction. "Why are you angry at her?" they asked.

He replied with pain, "Obviously, how would you know? Even Henry didn't know this, and he may not believe me."

Henry looked confused and concerned. "What? What don't I know, and what won't I believe?"

"That, I was killed... it was a murder, and the person who killed me was no one else but your beloved mother."

Henry's eyes widened in disbelief. "No, how could that be possible...?"

"I knew you wouldn't believe me, which is why I told you earlier that you wouldn't. Beta, this is the truth you've been hidden from. There's more I discovered before coming inside this casket. Your mother was having..."

"Having what?" Henry's voice trembled.

"An affair with Joseph. You may remember that when your mother died, Joseph brought her body, crying crocodile tears to show pain, but he had killed her. Joseph filled Stuti's ears with lies, which led her to kill me. I tried to give you hints many times, but you couldn't find them. Do you remember the night before you came here?"

"Yes, that night... I remember it well."

"A woman was killing a man on the street. It was your mother and me, flashbacks of the night she killed me there."

"Sorry for interrupting, but how is your casket here?" Aayan asked.

"There is a reason behind it," Edward replied. "Joseph was given room no. 105, through which you came here. He performs black magic, and he created the way through an almirah to this place. Because of his powers, Stuti wrote the book so well."

"Oh, that's a point!" Daisy exclaimed.

"So, what was Joseph's actual aim?" Roy asked the soul.

"It remains a mystery to me. I don't know clearly, but I might help you if you tell me about his behaviour now," Edward suggested.

"Yes, of course, we can," Aayan said. "He wore a mask before. Henry, do you remember this?"

"Yes, Dad, I do. I used to wear one just because of him. He told me to do so, but I never

understood why he wanted me to follow his instructions so blindly," Henry replied.

"Okay, that's all I wanted to tell you. Firstly, he will bring you under his control and then, when his work is done, he forgets everyone who helped him and even kills them, like your mother, Henry. The best result will come if you answer these questions correctly. I know the result but..."

"But what?" they all asked, looking at each other with anticipation.

"But I can't tell you until you complete all these questions. Otherwise, it won't work," Edward said.

"Okay, no problem. We will try to complete it, don't worry," Roy reassured him.

"Okay, I can help you answer the third question properly," Edward offered.

"Thank you, you are the best," Trisha said gratefully.

Chapter-17

Mr Edward began explaining the answer to the third question, "As you already know, Henry is my son, but the room was not mine."

"Then whose room was it?" Roy screamed his voice filled with urgency and confusion.

"It belonged to David's father. Do you remember David?" Edward's voice trembled slightly, hinting at the gravity of the revelation.

"No..." Trisha said hesitantly, her brows furrowed as she tried to recall.

"Wait, wait, and is he our vice principal?" Aayan interjected, his eyes widening in shock and disbelief.

"Yes, you are right. It belonged to his father. Later, one day he had a heart attack; he was already suffering from heart disease. Joseph knew about the room, and after the deaths of David's father, Stuti, and me, he took control of the school. David settled in Baddi, in District Solan, near the famous Vardhman factory. When he left, he entrusted the keys to Henry because I and his father were good friends."

"Then why did he become vice principal at our school? Did he lose his job or something else?" Daisy asked her curiosity piqued as she shrugged her shoulders.

"There is a reason behind it. The job he had in Baddi, the building caught fire accidentally, and many people lost their lives. Fortunately, David escaped safely," Mr Edward explained, his voice filled with sorrow for the victims.

"Thank God, he is alive," Daisy sighed with relief, her tension easing slightly.

"Yes, I was also so happy to see that. Okay, now you may enter the answers to the questions in the book you have," Mr Edward said with a reassuring smile.

"Yes, I totally forgot about it. Thank you for reminding me," Aayan replied gratefully.

They all formed a circle around the book as Aayan began writing the answers. The first answer froze as before, and now only one question remained. Their excitement grew as they planned to find the answer to the second question.

Edward started to tell them about Joseph. "He was a wonderful man from my perspective, at least initially. He had the best personality in the school—his communication skills, dressing sense, and way of walking were impeccable. I thought I knew him well when he first arrived. But later, I began to have my doubts. He would often ask me about my daily routines, my office, and the places I frequently visited. I ignored it at first, dismissing it as harmless curiosity."

He paused, his face clouding with a mix of regret and anger. "Only once did I see my wife talking to him, just days before my murder. I wasn't aware of what was happening and didn't expect this betrayal. He also talked to David a lot, perhaps he saw him while coming and going, like you kids saw Henry. The school was once called the best in the world... But now, you can see what it has become."

The group listened intently, their faces a mixture of shock and determination. They knew they had to uncover the hidden truths to solve the mystery.

"If you had doubts, why didn't you decide to investigate?" Roy asked, shrugging his shoulders and glancing at each member.

"Yes, especially after you saw him with your wife," Aarya added.

"No, I didn't have doubts when he was with my wife because all the staff talked with each other. It seemed usual, so I didn't think much of it. Before I could understand anything, I was assassinated. It was only after my death that I realized the full extent of the betrayal," Edward explained, his voice filled with regret. "I felt regret after my death, but it had no value then."

"Could you please also tell us how you came to be here?" someone inquired.

"It is a long story, but I will tell you. I was twenty when my father died. He had a dream to make me the principal of a school, but before he could do anything, he also died. I fell into depression for about a year, but at twenty-one, I realized that the responsibility was mine to look after my family. Then, I purchased this land to open a school. Every room was made under my supervision. This is why I knew the location of each room so well. After all, as I built the school, I was the owner of the land, and it was only fitting that I became the principal of the school. This is how I reached here, and the school was named after my grandmother, Mary, a Christian, hence St. Mary."

The group listened intently, feeling a mix of admiration and sadness for Edward's story. They understood the weight of his journey and the legacy he had left behind.

"Okay, okay, it is good to listen to your story, but can we move back to the point?" Henry asked seriously, but he burst into laughter at the end.

"Yes, yes, why not. It is more important to you, but I told you as much as I remember and know about him. Now you may go and learn more from David," Mr Edward replied.

"Yes, we will go, but..." Daisy hesitated, looking down at her foot.

"But... but what?" Trisha asked her curiosity piqued.

"It would be better if you come with us, Mr Edward, right Daisy?" Roy suggested, understanding Daisy's hesitation.

"Yes, you got the point!" Daisy exclaimed, her eyes lighting up.

"But how can I come? I would..." Mr Edward began to protest, but Henry interrupted, "You can, and you might tell us the way back to the school since you know it well. Please, Dad, can't you come with your son to help him?"

Edward paused, the room falling into a heavy silence for two minutes. Then, breaking the stillness, he said, "Okay, I will come."

Chapter-18

They all started moving back towards the school, guided by Edward, who knew all the ways.

"Aayan, could you please go to Joseph and hear his plans or discussions? It might help us," Edward suggested, as he assured them he would be invisible to anyone except them six.

Edward agreed and went to Joseph's office. He found a diary Joseph was reading and began reading it from the page Joseph had left off. As he read through the diary, he learned about Joseph's ambitions and plans. After absorbing all the information, Edward rushed back to the group. They were with David, inquiring about Joseph's aims, and were surprised to see that David could see Edward.

After their discussion, they discovered Joseph's aims: "The present principal of St. Mary, Mr Joseph, aims not only to become the principal and kill its owner but to become the head of Shimla, then the state, India, and finally the whole world."

They also found out from the diary that Joseph had a secret room outside the school campus, under a small shop opposite the main gate. In that room, he had all the tools to perform black magic and dolls representing every teacher and student. However, there was a way to destroy it all by sprinkling Gangajal on the main place where he worshiped the devil.

After learning this, they forgot about the book and its answers and went to their room, 105. They decided to sprinkle Gangajal, and fortunately, Henry had a little with him. Since students were not allowed to go outside the campus, Henry and David had to do it alone, but the others' wishes and support were with them.

They devised a plan that should work perfectly. The next day, they five stayed in the room while Henry and David went outside, disguising themselves as saints to avoid suspicion. As they stepped outside, Edward arrived to remind them, "It is 12 noon, and according to the diary, Joseph would be at home now. I think you should use plan B instead of plan A; it would be better."

They nodded and moved forward but asked Edward to check if Joseph was in the room or not before proceeding.

But Edward didn't because he is a soul and couldn't go to such places, so he went back. They looked at each other and nodded their heads to move forward. They started singing a bhajan, "*Mere Ghar Ram Aaye Hai,*" at the shop on the roadside and then took a one-rupee coin in their hand. Then, they moved downstairs into the room and started singing the song again in front of the main door.

Inside, Joseph, in his real form, was performing rituals on a doll. He got distracted when they rang the bell of his home. He stood up in anger and opened the door. They were surprised to see him in black clothes with white dots on his cap and clothes. They stopped singing, and their faces remained in shock. Silence lingered for approximately two minutes, but Joseph broke it.

"What do you want?" he said in anger. When no reply came, he added, "Are you deaf or here to disturb me?"

Henry replied, "We... we are saints, and today is our Guru Ji's birthday..."

As they were completing, Joseph said with anger in his eyes, which seemed to be red, "Then... then what can I do? You want me to celebrate his birthday or something else?"

"No... No, we didn't mean that. We just need you to let us inside and give us some food to eat."

"Oh, something else," he said with sarcasm and added, "See, I don't have time, and I'm so busy."

"Okay... even please give us some water to drink," David said immediately.

Joseph was irritated but said yes. As they entered inside, they saw that place. It was right in front of them. As Joseph went inside, Henry took out Gangajal, and as he sprinkled it, Joseph saw everything getting destroyed and scattered in the atmosphere. Everything was destroyed within a few seconds in front of their eyes, and Joseph couldn't do anything. He screamed in anger, and by then, they ran from there.

He chased them in anger, intent on killing them. Henry realized that they hadn't filled in the answer to the third question and knew it had the best result after doing this. Fortunately, Edward appeared, and Henry told him about it. While Henry and David were escaping from Joseph, the five were filling in that long answer in the book.

All were in a whirl, and there was a threat to Henry's and David's lives. As Joseph drew nearer, the school campus began to tremble violently as if a major earthquake had occurred.

Epilogue

They were astonished to see that it wasn't just an earthquake. The souls they had seen in the hidden room were now flying through the sky, and the dust swirled and settled in the corners. Before they could comprehend the situation, Edward arrived with the five students and told Henry and David that they had filled in the answers in the book, which might explain the current events. Joseph had never expected that they could solve the book's riddles since he had confided in no one except David and his diary, mostly the diary. Confused and with a softened heart, he retreated to his office.

While Joseph sat in his office, crying, Henry, David, and the others confronted him. The argument lasted over half an hour, with Henry and David accusing Joseph of his intentions to rule the world and become like Hitler. Eventually, Joseph asked, "How did you come to know about it? I hadn't told anyone."

Henry replied with a sarcastic smile, "Do you know Stuti... someone's wife..."

Joseph was shocked. "How did you come to know about it?"

"By Edward," the five students said as they stepped forward.

"You... you are those stupid kids. Huh?" Joseph said angrily.

"Yes, we are. If you don't believe us, Edward is still here," Aayan said, clapping his hands to reveal Edward to Joseph.

"Oh my god, what is this?" Joseph remarked, bewildered.

They explained everything to Joseph, and he was finally handed over to the Shimla Police as a criminal at the school. As Joseph crossed the road where the school's boundary ended, the school transformed back to its former glory, just as it was when Edward was the principal. The children returned, everything normalized, and the school regained its worldwide fame.

With this, all traces of black magic disappeared, and Mr Edward's soul finally found peace. Parents were able to reunite with their children, and the five students continued their studies until graduation. They frequently returned to meet Henry and David, and it was heart-warming to see the school thriving even after a century.

The friendship between the group lasted their whole lives, a testament to their courage and unity. They became legends, their story told to generations of students who attended the school. St. Mary's School stood as a beacon of excellence, its legacy of overcoming darkness and embracing light etched into its very foundation.